nickelodeon

SpongeBob SQUAREPANTS™

Top of the Class!

By James Killeen • Illustrated by Heather Martinez

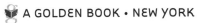 A GOLDEN BOOK • NEW YORK

Stephen Hillenburg

www.randomhouse.com/kids
Library of Congress Control Number: 2010922752
ISBN: 978-0-375-86568-8
Printed in the United States of America
10 9 8 7 6 5 4 3 2 1

Business was booming at the Krusty Krab. "Hurry up with those Krabby Patties!" yelled the owner, Mr. Krabs.

"I'm a Krabby Patty machine!" replied the fry cook, SpongeBob, who was working harder than ever to fill the many orders.

Plankton, the evil owner of the Chum Bucket restaurant, watched from across the street.

"They have so many customers!" he exclaimed. "I must steal the secret Krabby Patty formula and put the Krusty Krab out of business—once and for all!"

So Plankton created a wonderfully evil plan. It started with a disguise. . . .

The next day, a tiny green salesman visited Mr. Krabs.

"Boy, do I have a deal for you, Mr. Krabs. This machine can make five thousand Krabby Patties a day."

Plankton's plan was working perfectly. Now he just had to trick SpongeBob into giving him the Krabby Patty formula.

"Take this textbook, Mr. SquarePants," instructed Plankton. "Classes in pattyology begin tomorrow morning!"

"A master's degree in pattyology!
Textbooks! HOMEWORK!" cried SpongeBob.
"I LOVE SCHOOL!"

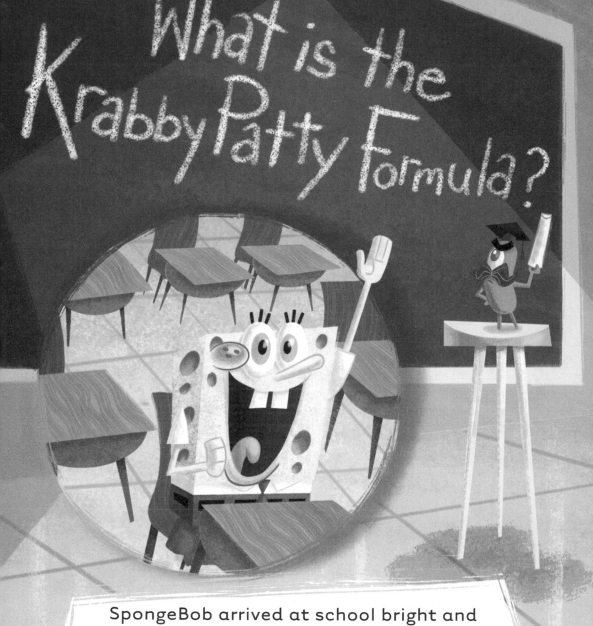

SpongeBob arrived at school bright and early the next day.

"Who would like to answer the question on the board?" asked Plankton.

"Me, MƐ, **MƐ!**" shouted SpongeBob.

"This is going to be harder than I thought,"
Plankton grumbled to himself.

"That's enough classwork," said Plankton.
"How would you like to try out the Krabby
Pattinator Five Thousand?"
"ARE YOU KIDDING?" screamed SpongeBob.

"Mr. SquarePants, please gather the Krabby Patty ingredients for me," said Plankton.

"Oh, I've already loaded the machine with the ingredients. I also woke up early and read the whole manual," declared SpongeBob.

"Let's make sure the mixture is correct," Plankton said, peering into the Krabby Patty machine. "Ah. Here we go!"

"Go?" said SpongeBob, hitting the Start button.

"Nooo!" yelled Plankton as he fell into the Krabby Pattinator 5000.

Plankton was not pleased.

"That's it! This isn't worth it! Class dismissed . . . FOREVER!"

Plankton pressed a button and the Krabby Pattinator 5000 blew to pieces.

SpongeBob was dejected. His dreams of school had been shattered!

"No classes! No homework! And worst of all, NO GRADUATION!"

Back at work, SpongeBob's job suddenly
seemed pointless. He could barely flip a single
patty. Mr. Krabs wished he'd gotten his free
machine. But even more, he missed having his
speedy fry cook.

"SpongeBob is the best fry cook ever to flip
for the Krusty Krab—and he's better than any
machine!" declared Mr. Krabs. Suddenly, Mr.
Krabs had a plan.

"Mr. Squidward, get to work inviting all
of SpongeBob's friends here tomorrow!"
"Why?" Squidward mumbled.
"Just do it!" Mr. Krabs shouted.

"Congratulations, SpongeBob! Based on your outstanding performance in the Krusty Krab kitchen, you have earned the first-ever degree in **FRY COOK MASTERY,**" announced Mr. Krabs.

SpongeBob was happy to be a master of fry cook arts. And he was even happier to have the best friends in Bikini Bottom!